DO YOU ENJOY BEING FRIGHTENED?

WOULD YOU RATHER HAVE
NIGHTMARES
INSTEAD OF SWEET DREAMS?

ARE YOU HAPPY ONLY WHEN
SHAKING WITH FEAR?

CONGRATULATIONS ! ! ! !

YOU'VE MADE A WISE CHOICE.

THIS BOOK IS THE DOORWAY
TO ALL THAT MAY FRIGHTEN YOU.

GET READY FOR

COLD, CLAMMY SHIVERS
RUNNING UP AND DOWN YOUR SPINE!

NOW, OPEN THE DOOR–
IF YOU DARE ! ! ! !

Shivers ™

THE SPIDER KINGDOM

M. D. Spenser

Paradise Press, Inc.

Plantation, Florida

To RSK,
a Spencer in his own right

Published by Paradise Press, Inc. by arrangement with River Publishing, Inc. All right, title and interest to the "SHIVERS" logo and design are owned by River Publishing, Inc. No portion of the "SHIVERS" logo and design may be reproduced in part or whole without prior written permission from River Publishing, Inc. An application for a registered trademark of the "SHIVERS" logo and design is pending with the Federal Patent and Trademark office.

ISBN 1-57657-102-5
30621

EXCLUSIVE DISTRIBUTION BY PARADISE PRESS, INC.

Cover Design by George Paturzo
Cover Illustration by Eddie Roseboom

Printed in the U.S.A.

Chapter One

"Someday, Freddy, you're going to get caught in a web of your own lies," Mr. Diplinger boomed at me in his deep, echoing voice. "You're going to get tangled up in all the things you've done wrong!"

Mr. Diplinger was the principal of our school, a large man with a heavy black mustache and thick glasses that magnified his eyes.

I was in his office — in trouble. Again.

My best friend, Lumpy, was with me. He's a bad dude — real mean and nasty, the biggest bully in the school.

But Lumpy doesn't try to push me around. Probably because we both like to have the same kind of fun. The kind that got us into trouble at school that afternoon.

It wasn't any big deal. So what if we set off a few firecrackers in the boys' bathroom? As if anyone really cared.

The explosions were way cool. Kids jumped all over the place, trying to get out of the line of fire. And nobody got hurt, anyhow.

"But Mr. Diplinger — like I told you, Lumpy and I just walked into the bathroom when someone else set off those firecrackers," I lied. "I *am* telling the truth! We didn't have anything to do with it!"

"Yeah. And it was a good thing we were lucky enough not to get hurt, ourselves!" Lumpy said with a goofy grin. "My mom makes me stay away from firecrackers on account of they could put my eye out or something."

Mr. Diplinger frowned, his huge eyes staring down at us through the heavy lenses.

"We have three students who saw you boys light two packs of firecrackers and throw them toward someone!" the principal barked. "Now do you want to keep lying to me or tell me the truth?"

"Who saw us throw them firecrackers? I'll beat him for ratting on us!" Lumpy shot back, without thinking.

"Oops," I said under my breath. "Nice going, Lumpy."

Lumpy got his nickname because he is very big and very fat. His stomach sticks way out over his belt. He's a good fighter, though, weighing three times more than any other kid in the school.

All Lumpy has to do is sit on his poor opponent to win.

No one ever said he was smart. Lumpy doesn't like to think much — and he proves that almost every time he opens his mouth.

Lumpy's stupid confession resulted in a three-day suspension from school for both of us.

As punishment, he was beaten with a leather belt by his mother. He told me it didn't even hurt.

My parents just yelled a lot. And they grounded me, saying I couldn't leave our yard until I returned to class.

As if I cared what they said! After they left

home for work, I went wherever I wanted anyway.

So everything turned out OK, really. Lumpy and I had three days off from school, and nothing to do except run around our neighborhood together.

We both lived in a new subdivision outside the city, at the edge of the woods. The builders were putting up houses all around us, constantly digging and hammering and sawing.

So, during our suspension, we pushed over stacks of bricks piled around the vacant lots. We snuck inside half-constructed homes to write our initials on the walls. And we stole enough lumber to make our own tree fort in the woods.

Hey, so what if we ran off with a few dozen boards? It's not like the builder can't afford it, you know?

Why should I care about some rich guy who makes a fortune selling new homes?

My parents said they didn't understand why I liked to cause so much trouble. But it's not like I was a bad kid or something.

I didn't use drugs or drink alcohol or anything

really dumb like that.

It's just that I was twelve years old and wanted to have a good time. Lumpy was the same way, only he was thirteen.

I learned a lot from hanging out with an older kid like him.

"You've got to throw your weight around if you want to have any fun, Freddy!" Lumpy always said to me.

He meant that it was always better to have a laugh at the expense of someone else — as long as our victim was powerless to fight back!

I pretty much agreed with him, though I thought sometimes Lumpy went a little too far.

When we were building the tree fort, for example, we saw an orange butterfly floating through the woods toward us. I liked watching it flutter along on those thin, fragile wings, soaring with the breeze.

I'm not a sissy or anything, but butterflies really are beautiful to look at, you know.

Lumpy just grabbed a big board and smashed the butterfly, as if he were hitting a baseball. The little thing just sailed into the trees in a tiny, dead heap.

"Why'd you do that?" I asked him, annoyed.

"Hey, why not?" Lumpy answered. "Who cares?"

I decided he was probably right. Why should I worry about a stupid little butterfly?

The only bugs I really enjoyed killing were spiders.

I *hated* spiders!

The way they creep around, crawling across everything with those eight gross legs! Yuck!

They made me sick.

I hated to admit it, but the truth was that spiders scared me to death.

I thought I was pretty brave for my age most of the time. I was tall and stronger than a lot of the kids. Spiders were the only things that made my flesh turn pale and cold with fear.

So I went out of my way whenever I saw one to step on it with my shoe, or squash it with a magazine or something.

I just didn't ever want to touch one of those

ugly, disgusting beasts with my hands.

I wasn't like Lumpy, who caught daddy long-legs spiders and pulled off all their legs so they couldn't move. Man, sometimes I thought he was crazy!

But I didn't understand how crazy, until I saw him carrying something around that could have gotten both of us killed!

After we finished building our fort, it was quiet enough for a while. Lumpy and I just swiped some popcorn and colas from my kitchen and played poker for pennies all afternoon inside our new hideaway.

We brought along a green plastic flashlight and a long rope to our tree house, too — just in case we ever needed it for something. You could never tell what might come in handy.

This was the second day of our suspension. We were having a great time, laughing at our card games and throwing empty soda bottles into the woods.

Then Lumpy pulled something from his shirt pocket.

"Hey, I've been saving this all day for you, Freddy," he announced. "I found it in the woods yesterday when we were building the fort. But I knew you'd want it. Here, it's a gift."

"What is it?" I asked warily, knowing Lumpy would never give me a real gift.

"Just take a look," he said. He opened his hands to reveal a small, hairy, black spider.

"Oooooh, gross!" I protested. "Get that away from here! Put it down and let me smash it!"

"No way," Lumpy said, grinning and moving close to me. "He's *yours*! I want you to keep him as a pet!"

"Yeah, right!" I said angrily. "Get away from me with that thing, Lumpy!"

"I think he's kinda nice, Freddy. Let me put him right up by your face and — oh no!" Lumpy shouted. "*Oh no! Aaaaaagh!*"

And then he tossed the hairy spider wildly out of his hands — and right down the inside of my T-shirt!

"It's a black widow!" Lumpy screamed. "Look

out, Freddy! It'll kill you!"

I ripped frantically at my chest, trying to untuck the T-shirt from my pants to dump out the spider.

"Get it out of there before he bites you, Freddy!" Lumpy hollered. "He's probably really angry now!"

But the faster I tore at my clothes, the clumsier my hands became. And the more terrified I felt!

I grabbed and tugged and yanked at my shirt, but it was no use.

A deadly spider was crawling around on my chest, ready to strike at any moment!

And I was helpless to do anything but wait for the vicious creature to deliver its fatal bite!

Chapter Two

I jumped up so fast that I banged my head on the roof of our tree fort, desperate to get the black widow out of my shirt.

But I was so scared of the spider that I didn't even feel the pain in my head.

I just screamed at Lumpy.

"Help me! Help me, Lumpy!" I bellowed. "Get him out! Get him *out*! *Aaaaaaaggh*!"

Instead, Lumpy smacked me hard on the chest with his right hand.

Thwaack!

"Got him!" Lumpy said triumphantly.

Then he slowly untucked my shirt and dropped the dead spider into his waiting hand.

For some reason, the spider didn't look dead.

Then I noticed it didn't even look squashed.

And then I finally saw the truth: The spider *wasn't real!*

It was only a rubber spider with plastic hair.

Some joke, huh? Really funny.

"Lumpy you big, fat jerk!" I said, hitting him hard on the shoulder with my fist. But Lumpy is so heavy I don't think he even felt it. "You totally freaked me out, you moron! I should kill you!"

He was just laughing, practically doubled over in a gale of guffaws.

"*Ha, ha, ha, ha, ha, ha!* You should have seen your face!" he cackled. "You are so chicken when it comes to spiders! What a baby!"

"I am *not* a baby! I'll kick your big, fat butt right now, you jerk!" I responded angrily. "I just don't like spiders, is all. Big deal! Don't ever pull something like that on me again, Lumpy, or I'll break your teeth! I swear it!"

"Yeah, yeah, sure, sure. You and who else?" Lumpy said, still laughing. "Anyway, it was just a joke. Can't you take it? Remember what I always say: You've got to throw your weight around if you want to have any fun, Freddy."

"Yeah, well, you have enough of it to throw around, that's for sure!" I said, still fuming.

I rubbed my head. I had begun to feel the pain from bumping my skull on the roof.

"I almost banged my brains open, too." I said. "I was thinking about jumping out of this tree fort, you had me so freaked out. If I jumped from this far up, I'd probably break my back or something. Then how would you feel, you idiot?"

"I'd feel fine, as long as it wasn't *my* back! But *you* wouldn't feel so good," Lumpy laughed. "Come on, you pansy! Forget about it! You're all right. It's just a little plastic spider. Here, you can keep it."

"No, thanks. I don't want it," I answered, staring down at the fake creature. "That's so gross! Besides, black widows don't have any hair! I should have remembered that from science class. You're so stupid!"

"And you're such a sissy!" Lumpy replied.

We often insulted each other like this. I'm not sure why — just something Lumpy and I did to annoy each other. Hey, why not?

I guess it probably hurt his feelings when I called him fat and stupid.

I have to admit that it made me feel a little bad, too, when Lumpy called me names like sissy or pansy. Even though I understood I was really not a sissy, you know. Because he said the same thing over and over, he almost got me wondering about it sometimes.

But I figured, fair is fair and if he wanted to insult me, he was going to get it right back.

If Lumpy didn't care how I felt, why should I care about him, right?

We just stood around the tree house now, still irritated with each other and not saying a word. Then Lumpy saw something that made us both feel better.

A victim!

It was Tommy Malloy, the best kid to pick on at our school. What a geek!

He's a small little nerd with big brown glasses and a huge nose. Malloy gets straight A's in all his classes but he's too little to fight. And besides, Malloy says he doesn't like fighting anyway.

The twit!

Tommy Malloy was the kid we attacked with firecrackers in the school bathroom. I didn't want to hurt him or anything, really — but it was cool to see this geek run around terrified while firecrackers exploded like some machine gun.

He was scared to death!

Lumpy and I climbed down the ladder of our tree fort and stopped Tommy Malloy as he walked home from school. This was going to be good.

"You told on us, didn't you, Malloy?" Lumpy said, pushing the frightened kid. "You ratted on us and got us suspended from school? I ought to pound you good for that one, you little fink!"

"Yeah, Malloy — it had to be you!" I said, playing along with Lumpy. I didn't really think Malloy told the principal about us, but this was too much fun to pass up.

"I — I — uh, I didn't say a word about it. Honest," Malloy stammered. "I didn't tell anyone! It, uh, must have been, uh, somebody else, guys!"

"Yeah, says *you*!" Lumpy responded.

"Yeah, we think you're lying, Malloy!" I said.

We grabbed the terrified kid's books and tossed them into the woods — then Lumpy socked Malloy once, hard in the stomach.

The little baby almost started to cry!

"Ha, ha, ha!" Lumpy laughed. "Run on home to do your homework, geek."

"Yeah, go play with your computer, Malloy," I shouted, laughing along with Lumpy. "You computer nerd!"

Actually, I guess I was kind of a computer nerd, too. I really enjoyed working on my dad's computer at home. And I was pretty good at it.

I even thought I might want to become some kind of computer scientist when I grew up.

But Lumpy didn't know that, and neither did Tommy Malloy. I wasn't about to tell them, either.

After we finished taunting this scared kid, Lumpy and I climbed back into our tree house and each drank about our sixth or seventh cola. The end of a perfect afternoon.

"Man, that was fun. What a pansy that guy is,"

Lumpy laughed.

"Yeah, he's a little jerk," I agreed. "It's always funny to watch him try to get away from us before you belt him. Hey, but you don't think you really hurt him any this time, do you?"

"I dunno. Who cares?" Lumpy answered, gulping from his soda bottle. Sticky cola dribbled down his fat chin. "What can he do about it anyway? All I know is, it's fun to watch him run away from me. It makes me feel good to see the little baby get so scared."

"Yeah, me too!" I said. But I was lying.

Really, I just thought it was funny to pick on Tommy Malloy. It didn't seem like any big thing to me. I never felt good about it — or bad about it either, for that matter.

Teasing kids like Malloy just seemed to be something fun to do. A way to "throw your weight around," as Lumpy said.

Unfortunately, Lumpy's weight was about to cause us a horrible problem.

We were sitting in the tree fort, playing cards

and laughing about Tommy Malloy, when I heard something.

Krrrreeeeaa!

"What was that?" I asked Lumpy, looking around.

"Huh? What are you talking about? I didn't hear nothing," Lumpy said, stuffing popcorn into his mouth as he talked. "Just play your cards."

Krrrreeeeaa!

"There it is again," I said. "You didn't hear that?"

"I didn't hear any sounds," Lumpy replied. "Are you gonna play cards or what?"

Krrrreeeeaa! Krrrreeeeaa!

There was a pause. This time even Lumpy heard it. He looked up from his bag of popcorn.

Krrrreeeeaa! Krrrreeeeaa! Krrrreeeeaa!

"Hey, what *is* that?" Lumpy asked, looking worried. "It sounds like something creaking."

"No kidding, stupid," I said. "But what is it?"

Then in an instant, I knew exactly what had made the sound: The tree house was breaking apart

17

under the strain of our weight.

We hadn't built the fort with the right kind of wood — and now it was ready to collapse under us!

Krrrreeeeaa! Krrrreeeeaa! Krrrreeeeaa!

We were thirty feet in the air, with nothing below us but a couple of branches and a long drop to the rock-hard ground.

I knew if the fort gave way, the fall could kill us!

There was little time to get away! The wood was going fast!

Krrrreeeeaa! Krrrreeeeaa! Krrrreeeeaa!

"Don't move! The fort's breaking up under us, Lumpy!" I shouted. "What are we going to do?"

Lumpy's eyes widened with fear, and pleaded with me to think of something. I could see he had no clue how to react. Lumpy was in a panic.

I couldn't think of anything, either — though I kept trying to figure some way out.

Suddenly it was too late!

Krrrreeeeaa! Krrrreeeeaa!

Krrraaaaacchh!

The floor under us cracked apart, creating an enormous hole!

And we were tossed, tumbling and screaming, toward almost certain death!

Chapter Three

Lumpy and I had fallen all the way through the floor of the tree house. We plummeted toward earth!

"Aaaaaaagggh!" he screamed.

"Aaaaaaagggh!" I screamed with him.

As I dropped, I managed to reach up with my hands and grab the large branch on which we had built the fort. I was just strong enough to hang on for dear life, with my feet dangling as Lumpy fell below me.

He plunged toward the ground with his back downward and his face looking up at the sky. He was still screaming. I felt certain my best friend was a goner!

"Luuummmpy!" I shouted.

When he landed, I started to laugh. I laughed so hard I almost couldn't hold on to the tree any longer.

Lumpy had not fallen to the ground. He had landed on a branch about ten feet below me — dropping safely onto a mass of soft, green leaves.

The branch bounced wildly when Lumpy slammed into it, but the sturdy old tree held. It was as if he had plopped onto a giant, gentle hand extended to rescue him.

"Are you OK?" I hollered. "I'm all right up here."

"Yeah, I guess I'm OK," Lumpy said, spitting out bits of leaves that had fallen into his open mouth. "Man, I thought we both were dead that time."

"We were really lucky, Lumpy! Really lucky!" I responded.

With a struggle, I hoisted myself onto the limb above my head, and sat there a few moments to rest. Then I crawled to the tree fort ladder and made my way to the ground.

Lumpy had a much tougher time getting down.

He was forced to sit sideways on the large branch, with his legs hanging down. Then, inch by inch, he slid his large rear end along the tree limb toward the ladder.

It was pretty funny to watch. I couldn't help laughing.

"Stop that! You're going to make me fall off if you keep making fun of me!" Lumpy complained.

I kept laughing anyway.

When he finally reached the ladder, Lumpy awkwardly twisted around on the branch, his chubby feet stretching to find the steps we'd nailed into the tree.

He clambered unsteadily onto the ladder and slowly climbed down. His hands were shaking.

"What's the matter, fatso? Get a little scared up there?" I asked with a laugh.

"Yeah, well, I heard you screaming just as loud, smart guy," Lumpy answered. "You wasn't exactly Batman up there, ya know."

Lumpy and I exchanged insults for a few minutes, then walked together toward our homes. Despite all the colas and popcorn, we both were hungry and ready for a snack.

Lumpy continued on his way home. I arrived in

my kitchen long before either of my parents would return from work. I knew they'd never find out that I had wandered outside the yard against their orders.

I opened the fridge to grab an ice cream bar — and that was when I saw it.

Mom had stuck a note for me on the freezer door, a note I hadn't noticed earlier when snatching the bottles of cola.

This is what the note said:

"Freddy, darling — Remember to stay in the yard! I don't want to find out you disobeyed us. And while you're home with nothing to do all day, please clean out the rafters around the entire front porch. They're a mess. Just use the garden hose. Thanks! Love, Mom."

The rafters? What could be wrong with the rafters over the porch, I wondered.

I'd never had to clean them out before, though I vaguely remembered Dad talking about doing it once or twice. He had mentioned something about some type of bugs up there, I recalled.

I knew I'd better get the chore finished before

Mom got home — otherwise she might ask questions about what I did during my second suspension day.

Quickly eating the ice cream bar, I walked toward the front porch, hoping to find nothing more than accumulated dust and dirt. I was afraid I might have to deal with a wasps' nest or two, spraying them with insecticide and then running like mad.

You can't just wash away a wasps' nest with the garden hose — but what does Mom know about that stuff, anyway?

When I opened the front door and looked out, though, I discovered something much worse than a couple of wasps' nests.

I'd rather have faced a dozen wasps' nests than what I saw up there.

Hanging over our porch, dangling from every rafter, were spiders.

Dozens of spiders.

Large brown spiders in their webs. Tiny black spiders suspended by single silken threads.

Spiders to my right. Spiders to my left. Spiders everywhere.

It was my worst nightmare come to life!

I felt as if every spider in the world was attacking my home, crawling over it, covering it with spider webs! And I had to defend the place all alone!

It was Freddy against The Great Spider Invasion!

And I knew just the weapon I had to use in order to fend off this terrifying assault!

Chapter Four

No way was I going to use some stupid garden hose to simply wash these zillions of monsters out of the rafters and onto the porch.

Gross!

I needed to *kill* the spiders. All of them.

I had to make absolutely certain every last one of those creepy, crawly bugs was stone-cold dead.

Sure, I could almost hear Mom saying what she usually told me about spiders: "They won't hurt you. And they're very good for the garden. I don't understand why you always kill the poor things."

Who cared about what she thought?

I didn't want to worry about dozens of spiders crawling around in our garden, just yards from the front porch.

I *hated* spiders! The only good spider was a

dead spider, as far as I was concerned.

Who cared about some stupid creature with eight legs? Especially one that might crawl over me in the middle of the night?

Haven't you ever awakened in the morning to find some little bump on your skin somewhere? And your parents say, "Oh, it's probably just a little spider bite." Like it's no big deal.

But to me, that meant some gross spider had been in my bed while I was asleep, sneaking around to attack me! How do they get under the covers anyway?

So I decided right then and there to forget the hose and go for the bug spray.

I ran into the garage and found a can of insecticide intended for destroying ants, wasps and spiders.

Then I sprayed everything in sight!

I sprayed and ran, sprayed and ran — trying to make sure no dead spiders dropped in my hair or anything.

The porch became obscured by a cloud of insecticide, a deadly fog that sent dozens and dozens of spiders to their doom.

I felt glad to see their little legs curl up as they died. Sometimes, though, a spider would survive the spray and try to crawl off toward the garden.

I always hurried to smash him with my foot.

In five minutes, dead spiders littered the porch. I got a broom and swept them into the lawn. Then I sighed with relief.

"Spiders! The disgusting little beasts!" I said. "What are they good for anyway? Well, at least now they won't be around to bite me during the night!"

Pleased with myself, I went inside, washed the spray off my hands and ate another ice cream bar.

It had been a busy day. Running around with Lumpy, hassling Tommy Malloy, falling from the tree fort, killing spiders.

Maybe I needed to lie down and rest a little before Mom and Dad got home, I thought.

So I flicked on the TV and stretched out on the comfortable leather couch in our living room, closing my eyes.

I would swear they weren't closed for more than ten seconds before I heard the strangest noise.

It was the sound of loud chomping and chewing, as if some glutton stood right in front of me, gorging himself on a snack. I could hear the rude slurping and sucking and swallowing, the grinding of hungry teeth, the licking of ravenous lips.

I wondered if Lumpy had sneaked into the house somehow and raided the fridge.

But when I opened my eyes, Lumpy was nowhere around.

Instead, I was confronted with the most shocking sight of my life!

Something so horrible, so unimaginable, that I wondered if I was losing my mind!

How was it possible?

Between the couch and the TV, a huge spider stood munching on an entire box of ice cream bars! A true monster!

He was at least five feet tall and very fat, weighing maybe two hundred pounds or more.

Something right out of a science fiction movie. Only he was no special effect!

The giant spider tore through the ice cream

bars one after another, ripping apart the paper with his fangs, gobbling the chocolate.

I screamed, shrinking back on the couch, trembling in total terror!

The spider kept gnawing at the ice cream, only glancing once or twice in my direction with his eight eyes.

The spider seemed to grow even fatter as I watched, each bite of food adding to his bulbous girth.

Suddenly, he looked right at me.

"Mmmmmmm," the monstrous spider said, a long tongue wiping his chops. "You look tasty."

I tried to get up off the couch, to run wildly hollering into the street. But my legs were frozen in fear.

"Get out of here! Get out of my home!" I yelled. "Heeeeelp! *Heeeeeelllp!*"

No one came. The spider just smiled, a stupid and goofy grin.

"Time for more food. You look like spider food to me, kid," he snorted.

"Get *away*! There's more food in the kitchen!

Eat anything you want! Just leave me alone! *Heeeeeeelllp!*" I bellowed.

"But why should I eat something else when it looks like so much fun to eat you?" the spider croaked. "You seem like there's good meat on you. And besides, what makes you think I would walk all the way to the kitchen for food — when *you're* right here?"

"There's, uh, lots of b-b-better stuff in the kitchen," I stammered. "Go look for yourself. Eat anything you want!"

"I want *yooou!*" the monster shouted. "You look much more exciting to eat than ice cream! So, you don't want to be eaten. Why should I care what you think? Remember, you've got to throw your weight around if you want to have any fun!"

With those words, the giant spider picked up his front legs and began to crawl slowly across the living room toward me.

One leg up and another leg down, step by step, the monster neared me.

I screamed one last time: *"Heeeeeeeeellp!"*

The spider closed his legs around me, opening his jaws for the first bite!

I could feel the beast touching me everywhere, its cold body against my quivering flesh!

I couldn't run! I couldn't hide! I couldn't even move!

I was about to become dinner for the ugliest, fattest, hungriest, most ghastly creature on earth!

<u>Chapter Five</u>

"*Wait*!" I screamed. "You can't be real! Spiders don't have teeth or tongues like yours! I remember that from my science class. And spiders certainly don't talk! You must be some kind of hallucination!"

"Does *this* feel like a hallucination?" the spider shot back, squeezing my ribs with his eight cold legs. "Do I look like a dream? Do I sound like a fantasy? Can you really believe these jaws ready to mash down on your head are only some illusion? You are very foolish, child, and I will teach you a lesson about reality you're not likely to forget!"

I knew at that moment that I was wrong: The spider *was* real! This horrible nightmare actually was happening to me.

I knew I had to think very fast if I was going to survive. I had to find some way to stall for time, hoping I'd find a way to escape from this freak of nature!

"You're right, spider. I am a foolish child. And obviously I know very little about spiders, despite my science teacher," I quickly responded. "So why not teach me a lesson about spiders before you eat me? Show me how spiders really live and how spiders really behave. I want to know the truth about spiders before I die. Please, spider, show me!"

The monster spider paused with his mouth open, as if unsure whether to eat me or grant my last request.

"Hmmmm," he finally answered slowly. "Perhaps biting into you just now isn't the best lesson after all! Perhaps, perhaps. Hmm, yes, perhaps it's worth the time to show you a thing or two before you become supper!"

The spider released his grip on my body, and walked around me in a large circle. As he walked, he spun a thick thread of silver silk, tying my arms securely against my chest. Soon, I was bound tightly, as if by a heavy rope.

"What are you doing, spider?" I asked, disgusted by the feel of the spider silk on my skin. "You don't need to tie me up. I'm not going to run away. Just let me go and I'll do whatever you want."

"So they all say. The flies tell similar lies, you know. As do the moths and mosquitoes," the giant spider said. " 'Just free me from your web and you can eat me whenever you like,' they plead with us. All spiders learn to see through liars. Now sit still and be quiet!"

The spider seemed very angry with my attempt to fool him. So I did as I was told, sitting still as the silk wound around and around and around my arms and chest.

When the spider finally finished, he stepped in front of me, admiring his work. His eight eyes examined the fresh silk thread, inspecting it to make sure I couldn't break free.

"Yes, it's tight. Yes, good and tight. That will do. Now stand and walk with me!" the spider commanded. "And try to keep up with me on your two puny little legs!"

Towing me like a prisoner being dragged in chains, the spider walked quickly through our home and out the front door. When he reached the porch, though, the spider suddenly paused.

"Here! Yes, it was *here*! The scene of the slaughter!" the huge spider bellowed. "Do you know how many spiders died senselessly on this porch from your poison spray? Fifty-three spiders lost their lives on this very spot! It was a mindless massacre — and all for nothing! When you could have washed every one of them harmlessly into your mother's garden with a hose! You *murderer!*"

No one had ever talked to me that way before — and certainly not a giant spider. My hands began to tremble and I could barely find enough voice to speak. I struggled to control my fear.

"I — I, uh — I'm sorry, spider," I said meekly. "I, uh, I guess I didn't think that — "

"You didn't *think* at *all!*" the spider thundered, interrupting me. "You never think, do you? You harm without any thought! Without ever considering the consequences of your actions! Well, come on, kid. Follow me now. You'll have time to think about your actions where I'm taking you."

The spider walked rapidly off, his legs rising and falling like the pistons of a huge engine, pulling me along behind. I had to trot to keep up.

"Spider, where are we going? Where are you taking me?" I asked desperately, puffing with fatigue.

There was only silence.

"Spider, please! Tell me where you're taking me! My parents will worry if I go too far from home," I pleaded. I could see now that we were headed toward the woods. "Besides, I'm grounded. I'm not supposed to leave our yard! I'm going to get into trouble!"

"Silence, child! You are already in trouble. Very serious trouble," the spider responded. "And anyway, it's not as if *you* care what your parents say. You don't worry about their orders to you, kid. You go where you want to go. And so you are free to follow me wherever I want to take you."

"But where is that, spider? You're frightening me. I just want to know where we're going," I whined. "Please, I'm *scared!*"

"I'm surprised you would ever feel scared, a big tough kid like you," the spider said sarcastically. "But I will tell you where we are going, since you finally admit you are frightened. Finally you tell me the truth about something!"

"Where? Where? Tell me, please!" I begged. "Where are we going, spider?"

"You are going with me to the great hall of our king!" the monster spider replied. "I am taking you to The Spider Kingdom!"

Chapter Six

"Wh-what did you say? Th-the spider what?" I squeaked.

"The Spider Kingdom, child!" the monster spider croaked. "Now start listening to what I tell you! And start thinking! You will soon be in the presence of our great king! We don't need any foolish kids offending His Highness!"

I screamed as loud as I could scream toward the houses of my neighbors, but no one seemed to hear me. Why didn't anyone come out to help free me? Why didn't someone at least call the police?

I struggled frantically to break free from my rope of spider silk but it was impossible. I was tied up tightly, with the spider dragging me toward the woods.

This still seemed crazy to me! How could

something so bizarre, so shocking, really be happening?

Maybe it was just a dream, I thought. Maybe it was only something I ate — my imagination twisted by too many colas and too much popcorn and ice cream.

Then I remembered the feeling of the spider's huge legs squeezing my ribs — and once again I knew that everything was all too real.

"Come along, kid! Hurry it up!" the spider commanded. "You certainly are a disgusting creature! The way you creep around, crawling across everything with those two gross legs! Yuck! You make me sick! Now hurry along, we need to move faster!"

The spider began to travel more quickly now, forcing me to run behind him. We raced down a path in the woods, toward the tree where Lumpy and I had built the fort. I prayed that somehow my best friend would be there, maybe patching up our broken hideaway.

I knew Lumpy would never let some monster drag me off into the woods. He would probably jump on the giant spider's back and beat the demon to death with a piece of wood.

He would save me!

I could see the shattered tree house now. But as the spider and I hurried past, there was no sign of Lumpy. I was alone, the prisoner of a killer beast!

I saw something large up ahead, as if we were heading for a cave of some kind. I knew these woods well — and I had never seen a cave in them before.

As we grew closer, I understood that it was not so much a cave as a hole. A vast, dark opening on top of the ground that became a deep shaft straight into the earth.

It was a huge spider nest!

Or a nest for huge spiders!

As my rope of spider silk pulled me toward the hole, I knew this was where we were going.

I was like a fly or a moth or a mosquito — just another helpless victim about to be lowered into a black and horrible world filled with hungry monster spiders!

Chapter Seven

I was surrounded by blackness.

The monster spider had tossed me over the side of the black hole — and now he was lowering me into the bottomless pit.

Suspended by only the single thread of spider silk, I felt sure this delicate rope would snap any second and I would plunge to my death. But the thread held and I descended further and further into the giant nest.

Finally, I saw a bit of light coming from below — then a little more light, then a little more. As the brightness grew, I watched myself approach the floor of the deep hole and felt my feet at last touch the earth again.

When I looked around, though, the sight was anything but comforting.

Spiders of all kinds swarmed around the massive nest, all of them at least as large as the giant that had brought me there. A mass of sticky white silk covered the walls of the hole. Strange candles illuminated the terrifying scene.

Looking closer, I saw the candles had been fashioned from the torn legs of spiders, wrapped in silk and lighted on fire.

"Ah reckon you've noticed the candles," a huge black spider said to me, speaking with a thick Southern accent. "How come you ain't laughin' no mo'? See, 'cause these here legs was ripped off our daddy longlegs friends by your buddy Lumpy and other kids just like him. Ah seem to recall you thinkin' that was pretty funny at the time."

"Well, uh — No, not really. I'm, uh — It's just, well . . . " I stammered, not knowing how to reply. I was afraid the wrong answer might get me killed! "Hey, *I* didn't do anything! I'm sorry about the legs, spider! But I didn't do it!"

"No, Ah know you weren't the one. You were too busy standin' around laughin' while ol' Lumpy did it, weren't ya?" the spider answered. "Oh, yeah, and sprayin' and stompin' on as many spiders as you could find. Yeah, sure, Ah recall you were plenty busy doin' that too, kid. Now, don't sass me no mo'! Ah know who you are! Jest shut up and follow me!"

The monstrous black spider shouted the final words. I shivered with fright. Panic surged through my body as the spider reached toward me with his long mouth, as if to take a bite out of my arms!

But he only chomped through the silken threads that bound me, freeing my arms, and then turned away.

"Come on with me, kid! Stay right close or you might get eaten by a hungry wolf spider!" he ordered. "We got all kinds of spiders in here — and some of them are mighty hungry for a good taste of a bad kid like you!"

"You must have the wrong boy, spider," I whined. "You don't want me! I'm not a bad kid! I don't want to hurt anyone. I don't do anything really wrong! I just like to have some fun!"

"Yeah, don't we all, kid? We all like to have

our fun, that's for shore," the spider responded. "Down here, we like to have a good time, too. Guess you could call it 'spider fun!' You'll just have to wait and see how you like it, though. See, 'cause sometimes what's fun for one particular somebody ain't so much fun for somebody else."

The spider tromped carefully through the silky, shadowy nest, which was a complex series of long tunnels. I followed closely behind him, watching constantly for anything that looked like it might be called a wolf spider.

As if I would have known a wolf spider from a tarantula, anyway. All I knew about spiders was that I despised them!

All the spiders in the nest looked alike to me. Each was huge and ugly and dark. Each stared hungrily at me with eight huge eyes, as if dinner was walking past.

Now and then, a spider clinging to the silken walls called out to me, with a mocking laugh: "What's wrong, kid? Lost your bug spray?" Or: "Hey, kid! Why don't you just step on us now?"

My spider guide and I trudged for what seemed like miles. Down this tunnel, through that tunnel and into another. On and on we walked, his eight legs rising and falling slowly as my two legs trundled along behind.

I rubbed my eyes, as though I still might awaken from a horrible nightmare. Nothing changed.

I remained deep inside the dark nest, surrounded by disgusting monsters.

I wasn't shaking or trembling or anything now. I must have been in shock. I was numb, as if someone had just knocked me on the head with a baseball bat.

I hardly even felt scared, despite the gross giant spiders everywhere.

Until I turned one corner — and saw a sight that made me shriek!

"*Aaaaaaaaagh!*" I screamed.

Right in front of me was my best friend, Lumpy — stuck in the netting of an enormous spider web!

He was trapped in the sticky web like a fat fly!

"Heeelp! Heeeelp me, Freddy!" he shouted wildly. "The spiders are going to kill me! *Heeeeeeeelllp!*"

Chapter Eight

It looked like Lumpy was about to become some spider's tasty tenderloin!

"Lumpy!" I shouted. "How did *you* get down here? You were going home after we left the tree fort. What happened? How did the spiders capture you?"

"Freddy, I never been so scared in my whole life. Help me, please!" Lumpy pleaded. "I wasn't doing nothing! I just went home and was eating a hot dog when this huge monster crashes through our kitchen window! He stuffs the hot dog in my mouth so I can't talk, then ties me up and drags me here! Now I'm stuck to this web and all these spiders want to murder me!"

"Why is this happening to us, Lumpy? We haven't done anything to deserve this," I said fearfully.

"We're just kids, Freddy! I'm scared of this

place. And all I want to do is go home!" Lumpy cried. "Where *are* we anyway? How can this be real? Maybe we're both going crazy!"

"Now you two boys already been told where ya are," the spider guide said irritably. "You kids better get the wax out of your ears and listen, 'cause I'm losin' my patience with y'all! This here's The Spider Kingdom, boys! Y'all are guests of His Highness, the Spider King!"

"Bu-but we, uh, don't want t-to be guests here," Lumpy stammered. "Thanks anyway. Can we go home now?"

"Noooooooo!" the spider guide bellowed angrily. "Y'all are gonna stay here until we're good and finished with ya! Get used to it, boys! This is your new home!"

I peered through the dark underground tunnel, watching the giant spiders crawl past us in the weird candlelight — and I nearly fainted. I couldn't believe I had to live in this awful place.

Lumpy and I might never see our own homes or our parents again!

"Let us go, spider!" I begged, falling on my knees. "Please, please, please, please let us go home! We'll do anything you want us to do! Honest!"

"Yeah, come on, spider! We've never done nothing to you," Lumpy whined, tears forming in his eyes. "Just let us go! We'll give you anything! My mom has some money in the bank. She'll give it all to you! Really she will!"

"Lies, lies, lies and more lies," the spider guide replied with an amused smile, shaking his head. "Y'all are good liars, you are. But then, guess you've had plenty of practice at it, huh? 'Sides, Ah don't want no money, kid! Ah want *yoooouuu!*"

"M-m-me?" Lumpy asked. "What's wrong with *him*?"

Lumpy was pointing at me! His *best friend!* I couldn't believe it.

"Hey, you jerk, he wasn't talking about me!" I said. "The spider was talking about you! You always were so stupid! He doesn't want me. He wants you!"

"Don't call me stupid, you pansy!" Lumpy snapped back. "If I wasn't stuck here in this web I'd break every single bone in your body! You've never had any . . . "

"Hush up, you two, or Ah'll eat both of ya myself right here and now!" the spider guide interrupted fiercely. "You boys surely do talk a blue streak! But ya have a long time to talk to each other now, that's for sure. So y'all can insult each other whenever the mood strikes. *Forever!*"

"Forever?" Lumpy blurted out, his lip quivering.

"Forever? What do you mean, 'forever,' spider?" I asked worriedly.

"Ah mean Ah got a job to do here, boy. And my job is to stick you to this here web with your fat friend!" the spider guide told me. "And once you're good and stuck, Ah got to walk away, see? 'Cause Ah been ordered to imprison the killer kids! That's what everyone calls y'all down here."

"Killer kids?" I gulped.

"Yep, you got yourselves in some bad trouble this time," the guide said. "See, you two are just gonna rot away on this here spider web. You're both gonna stay trapped right here, 'til there's nothing left of ya but your bones!"

Chapter Nine

I looked at Lumpy, who lay helpless across the massive spider web.

And I saw there was room for one more person.

Me!

I felt my knees buckle. Lumpy and I exchanged terrified glances.

What could I do?

There was nowhere to hide.

And if I ran, I would only get lost — and probably eaten by a wolf spider! Besides, the giant spiders were faster than I was, anyway. They would catch me in a matter of seconds and bring me back to the web.

The spider guide's eight eyes glared angrily at me. The spider began to move slowly toward me.

One leg up. Another leg down. One leg up. Another leg down.

The spider approached.

I backed up, step by step, edging as far away from this grotesque southern monster as I could.

"Leave me alone, spider! I haven't done anything!" I cried. "Leave me alone!"

Step after step after step, I walked backward. Step after step after step, I warily watched the spider guide crawl toward me.

Step. Step. Step. Step.

Then suddenly, it happened!

I backed up too far — right into the giant spider web!

I struggled with all my strength but couldn't budge. My arms wouldn't move. My legs wouldn't move.

I couldn't even turn my head.

I was just another human fly caught for the kill!

"Thank ya, kid!" the spider guide said. "I was hoping ya would do that so's I wouldn't have to get pushy with you. I hate gettin' pushy. Not all spiders like to fight, ya know."

The spider guide slowly turned now and, with black legs rising and falling, began to walk away into the shadowy tunnel.

"Oh yeah, boys! One thing I should mention, I reckon," the spider called out as he walked. "Y'all won't *really* stay stuck in the web forever and rot, like I said. I was just joking with y'all. Only a little spider fun. I know how y'all like to laugh so much. *Ha, ha, ha, ha, ha!*"

Still laughing, the black monster disappeared into the depths of the spider nest, leaving Lumpy and me alone, crying and uncertain of our fate.

We had no idea what would happen to us next.

Or when it would happen.

But we knew one thing — whatever happened, it wasn't going to be good.

And there was nothing we could do to stop it!

Chapter Ten

"What are we going to do, Freddy?" Lumpy asked. Tears streamed down his round cheeks.

"I don't know, Lumpy," I answered, tears coming from my eyes, too. "There's got to be some way out of here. We have to think of something — fast!"

"I don't know what to do. I'm just so scared," Lumpy said. "You're the smart one, Freddy. You can come up with some plan to save us! I — I'm sorry about what I said before, Freddy. You know, about you being a pansy and all. You're not really no pansy. I — I didn't mean it. Honest, I didn't, Freddy!"

"And I'm sorry for calling you stupid, Lumpy. Really I am," I said. "You're really not stupid."

"Oh, yes I am," Lumpy said sadly.

"No, you're not! You're just so busy picking

on everyone that you don't ever think about any-thing," I said. "You could be a lot smarter if you tried, Lumpy. You just never give your brain any practice, that's all. My dad always says anybody can be smarter if they really want to be. But I wish I was smart enough to figure out some way to escape from this hole. I can't move a muscle."

"I can't either, Freddy! I feel like I have ten kids holding me down," Lumpy said. "What do you think they're going to do to us? You think they're going to kill us? Maybe they're going to use us for food! I could feed a lot of spiders with all this fat."

"Hey, don't forget — I'm a pretty big kid for twelve years old! I could feed a few spiders myself," I said nervously.

Lumpy and I tried to look at each other but we couldn't even turn our heads an inch. Instead, I just moved my eyes to one side, catching only a blurry glimpse of the person trapped on the web beside me.

I tried to smile as bravely as possible, hoping to give myself some confidence. I sure needed it.

"It'll be OK, Lumpy," I said, not really believing my own words. "We'll get out of here somehow. I know we will. You'll see."

"You really think so, Freddy? Do you?" Lumpy said hopefully. "You think we're going to get out of this place?"

"Yeah, sure," I said. "I'm positive we'll get out of here. We'll think of something."

Actually, I did feel certain we would get out of the hole somehow. That part was the truth.

I just wasn't sure if we would be alive — or dead!

We lay spread-eagled on the sticky web for hours. Now and then, a huge spider would walk past us. Some were hairy and brown, others were smooth and red, and still others were long and black. They taunted us and jeered as they crept by.

"Having fun yet?" asked one brown spider with a laugh.

"Are you two still *hanging around*? Ha!" a red spider shouted.

"What are you kids doing there — surfing the web?" sneered a black one.

Lumpy and I grew so frightened we began to shiver, as if we were freezing, even though it really was kind of hot.

We were waiting to meet our fate — whatever it was going to be.

Two dark, furry spiders walked down the tunnel toward us, side by side. Their legs moved in perfect unison. It looked as if they were marching.

As they came closer, I heard one of them speaking, calling out to the other:

"Hip, two, three, four, five, six, seven, eight! Hip, two, three, four, five, six, seven, eight!" he repeated, like a sergeant in the army. "Company, *halt!*"

I saw that both spiders wore gold braids constructed of autumn maple leaf stems, with the commanding spider adorned by several more braids than his soldier.

"The prisoners are hereby informed that they are to be taken into the custody of the Imperial Guard," the company commander cried out. "The prisoners will refrain from any unnecessary conversation and make no attempts to escape, or be under pain of immediate execution!"

"Huh? What'd he say?" Lumpy whispered to me.

"He said we're being taken into custody and can't talk or try to escape," I answered. "If we do, they'll kill us!"

"Silence!" the commander screamed. "The prisoners will refrain from any unnecessary conversation!"

"But — but where are you taking us? What are y-you going to do with us?" Lumpy whimpered. "Don't hurt us! Please! W-we didn't do anything!"

"Silence, prisoner! You are in the custody of the Imperial Guard now! We are under orders to remove the killer kids from this prison web. That means you two must come with us," the commander barked. "And then we must escort the both of you to the court of the Spider King!"

<u>Chapter Eleven</u>

"Remove the prisoners!" the commander yelled.

"Yes, *sir!*" the soldier responded. He saluted strangely, raising both a right and left front leg to his eight eyes. "Right away, *sir!*"

The disgusting, hairy beast moved quickly to the prison web. Using his strong jaws, he sawed through the net to free Lumpy and me.

It felt good to be able to move. At least Lumpy and I were standing again, though our hair was still full of sticky spider webbing.

We had no idea, though, what might await us at the court of the Spider King.

We remained silent, as the commander had ordered us. We exchanged worried glances. Both of us grew more scared by the minute.

When I attempted to comfort Lumpy with a plucky smile, I found that I was too frightened even to force my lips to curl upward.

We were in deep trouble now — the worst of our lives. And both of us knew it.

"Guard, escort the prisoners!" the commander bellowed. "To the rear, *march!*"

The soldier moved behind us slowly and formally, then stood at attention with his eight legs perfectly straight. After yelling more orders, the commander led us away, the four of us marching off through the dark, long tunnel.

"Hip, two, three, four, five, six, seven, eight!" the commander barked, turning to look at us. "Stay in step, prisoners! Two steps for every one of ours! Inferior creatures! Hip, two, three, four, five, six, seven, eight!"

Lumpy and I struggled to march in time with the commander's calls, shuffling and skipping and half-stepping along to match the pace. But we were no good as soldiers and kept stumbling. Every time we faltered, the guard bumped into us from behind.

He snarled at us angrily, giving us each a hard shove.

"Move along, prisoners!" he growled.

"Stay in step!" the commander shouted.

We passed other spiders along the long march. They watched quietly as we passed. It was as if they knew better than to taunt us now, as if they were afraid to interfere with any prisoners in the custody of the Imperial Guard.

Down the spooky dark tunnels we marched, on and on, our way still lighted by candles made of torn spider legs wrapped in silk.

Our shadows flickered on walls plastered with white spider threads, casting strange and horrifying forms there — the darkened outline of a monstrous spider followed by the shapes of two trembling boys, with another gargantuan spider crawling along in the rear.

Sweat ran down my face. Lumpy puffed heavily from fatigue. I feared he might collapse and die before we ever reached the royal spider court.

"Hang on, Lumpy," I whispered. "We'll be

there soon!"

"I — I don't — whew! — don't know how much longer I can walk this fast," Lumpy panted.

"Silence!" the commander screamed. "The prisoners will refrain from any unnecessary conversation!"

Ahead, I saw two enormous doors made of great chunks of tree bark covered with green moss. On each side of the doors stood two soldiers, spider guards that wore a single circle of gold braid wrapped around every one of their legs.

As we approached, the four Imperial Guards raised their right and left front legs in a rigid salute to the commander.

"Sir!" they called out in unison. "His Majesty awaits the prisoners!"

"Company, halt!" the commander yelled.

Lumpy and I stopped walking, looking at each other with terror in our eyes.

We heard the sounds of a crowd gathered inside the court. Dozens of enraged voices screamed for our blood!

"We want the killer kids!" some of the voices shouted.

"Turn the killers over to us! We'll take care of them," other voices hollered.

"Murder the killer kids!" still other voices yelled.

A vicious mob was waiting for us! Who knew what would happen to us when we walked inside those huge doors?

"Announce the prisoners!" the commander ordered.

The Imperial Guards pushed open the doors and marched into the court. Lumpy and I could see hordes of furious spiders standing inside on a carpet of green leaves.

Lining both sides of the leafy rug, the crowd of spiders bayed and bellowed, many of them angrily raising their front legs as if preparing to pounce on their prey.

"Your Highness, if we may be allowed to speak," the four guards said together. "The commander of the Imperial Guard wishes us to convey this news: The prisoners are prepared for their appearance at the Royal Court whenever Your Majesty wishes!"

"Bring in the prisoners!" a deep, booming voice said. The crowd cheered. "Bring them inside the court! And I shall let my subjects decide if these killers should live — or if they should die!"

Chapter Twelve

Lumpy and I shuddered. A cold chill ran through my veins.

"Death! Death! Death! Death!" screamed the spider subjects. "Death to the killer kids!"

"Bring in the prisoners!" the booming voice repeated. "Bring them to the Spider King! I want to see their faces! Bring them in at once!"

The four guards marched together back to the doors, standing at attention, two on each side of the court entrance.

"Prisoners, *march*!" the commander bellowed.

Escorted by the Imperial Guard, we walked timidly into the court of the Spider King.

This royal place was entirely green: The walls, like the doors, were coated with a thick, fuzzy layer of moss. A vaulted ceiling of green sticks arched high overhead, with blades of grass laid across them to form a covering.

The leaves that served as a carpet were soft. Our footsteps made no noise as we trudged with dread toward the king. Daddy Longlegs candles burned everywhere around the hall.

His Highness was the largest, hairiest spider we had seen, a tarantula resting across an elevated throne of pine needles, his legs folded under him. He had a strange dark mustache and he peered at us contemptuously with his eight eyes, huge eyes that seemed as if they were magnified to look more intimidating.

He wore a long robe made of spider silk and a crown of twigs with bits of green leaves placed into it like jewels.

The mob of spiders to our sides shook their legs at Lumpy and me, jeering and shouting for our deaths, as we walked closer and closer to the king.

We were very near the throne. The Imperial Guard commander called for us to halt. He and the soldier stepped to one side, waiting at attention for the words of their king.

The mob fell silent. His Majesty studied us from on high, his eyes monstrously large.

"Bow down before royalty, insolent prisoners!" the king suddenly shouted. "Do you know where you are? Fall to your knees when you come before this court!"

The Imperial Guard commander immediately slapped at our feet with one of his front legs.

Lumpy and I shrieked — and dropped to our knees.

"Y-yes, Your M-Majesty," I stammered. "Forgive us. We meant no disrespect."

"S-sorry, King! We d-didn't mean nothing," Lumpy said, bowing as deeply as his fat stomach would allow.

"Do you know where you are, prisoners?" the king asked. His deep voice echoed off the walls of the vast green hall.

"Y-yes, Your Majesty," I said haltingly. "We are in the court of the Spider King, Your Highness."

"And do you know who I am?" the king inquired.

"Uh, yes, sir. That is, yes, Your Majesty. You are the Spider King," I replied.

"And do you know *why* you children are prisoners in the court of the Spider King?" the monarch asked.

He leaned forward to gaze down at us with a menacing look.

Lumpy and I turned to each other. Lumpy shrugged his shoulders helplessly.

"Y-you tell him, Freddy," Lumpy whispered, his voice quivering with fear.

"Uh — your honor, uh, that is I m-m-mean Your Highness, forgive us. We, uh, do not know why we are here, Your Majesty, sir. No, s-sir," I stuttered.

"Um, Your Highness, sir — I just thought of something," Lumpy said. "Are we here on account of the way Freddy hates spiders and all? 'Cause if that's it, well, sir, I shouldn't be here at all. I just want to say that I've always really, really liked spiders a lot, I and really want . . . "

"Silence, prisoner!" the king roared. "We will

hear no more of your lies! You have no regard for anything but yourself, and your behavior shows you even have little of that! Neither of you children care how much you harm any living creature! You destroy without thought! And now your destruction will be punished!"

B-but sir, Your Majesty," I said fearfully. "We weren't trying to hurt anything. I don't know what we did, but I know Lumpy and I must have been just having some fun. We're just kids! What could we have done that's so bad? We don't know anything!"

"You are both old enough to know better!" the king shot back. "You are both old enough to understand the consequences of your actions! A person without feelings for the suffering of others is likely to cause more suffering than he knows!"

"B-but what, uh, what have we done so bad, Your Honor, sir?" Lumpy stammered.

"Guard! Read the charges," the king commanded.

From behind the throne, a small yellow spider emerged, dragging a rolled-up elm leaf. The spider unfurled the leaf with his front legs, laid it across the floor and stood over it, reading aloud:

"To the prisoners known among humans as the children Freddy and Lumpy, the charges are as follows," the guard read. "For the recent needless chemical massacre of fifty-three spiders on his parents' porch, Freddy is charged with murder. For the senseless killing of one hundred twenty-one spiders that were existing peacefully and harmlessly outdoors, Freddy is charged with murder. For the mindless torture and death of ninety-five daddy longlegs spiders by amputating their limbs with his fingers, Lumpy is charged with murder."

The guard paused to clear his throat, choked up by reading this list of crimes.

"Go on," the king commanded.

"Furthermore, on behalf of all peaceful creatures, beast or man, His Majesty charges the prisoners with the following acts of unthinking cruelty," the guard continued. "For the merciless misery caused to schoolmate Tommy Malloy by numerous mean-spirited pranks, Freddy and Lumpy are each charged with brutality. For countless acts of bullying and harassment of more than a dozen other students, Freddy and Lumpy are each charged with brutality. Thus end the charges."

"How do the prisoners plead?" the king asked, staring at us angrily with his eight magnified eyes.

"Uh — sir, I guess — Well, Your Majesty, not guilty, sir," I said. "Right, Lumpy?"

"Um, yeah, sure, sir. Not guilty, Your Honor," Lumpy added. "We didn't do nothing."

"Very well," the king said gruffly. "The prisoners plead not guilty. We will let you make your case before the court of the Spider King. You can offer into evidence every fact that may tend to prove your innocence, prisoners. You may speak as long as you like in your own defense."

The king paused, frowning, his huge eyes furious.

"And then we will sentence you both to death," the king howled. "And this assembly of subjects will watch as the Royal Executioners destroy you with all the cruelty you deserve!"

Chapter Thirteen

"Death?" I cried.

"Death? Is that what he said, Freddy?" Lumpy asked, tears forming in his eyes. "B-but, Your Honor, sir, I . . ."

"The prisoners *will* be *silent*!" the king shouted. "You will not speak until spoken to! Bring out the Royal Prosecutor! Let her make the case against the prisoners!"

In the back of the huge hall, the two doors opened. A massive black widow spider slowly entered to cheers from the crowd. The prosecutor acknowledged the applause with a nod, and walked toward the throne with small, stately steps.

She took her place before the king, bowing to His Majesty, then turned to face Lumpy and me.

Her eyes turned cold and mean.

"Your Highness, with your permission I will make this case a brief one," the Royal Prosecutor announced in a regal British accent. "The facts are quite clear, I should think. The callousness and cruelty of these two defendants are recognized throughout your realm. The prisoners are even appropriately known among your subjects as 'the killer kids.' "

"Please, madam, do keep your remarks as brief as possible," the king agreed. "Our Royal Self would like to dispense with this unpleasantness as quickly as possible. It's all so distasteful, isn't it?"

"Indeed, Your Majesty. *Most* distasteful, sire," the prosecutor said, strutting back and forth before the throne as she spoke. "The prosecution believes that the most important points in this case are the following, Your Highness: The defendant known as Freddy has willfully ignored information about spiders that he was taught in school, information that should have allayed his unnatural fears of our species. The defendant known as Lumpy received the same information in his schooling — and likewise ignored it. These two people remembered nothing of the good spiders routinely do for human beings, including feeding on insects harmful to human gardens. As a result, the defendants have treated spiders as dangerous creatures, worthy only of destruction."

The mob of spiders let out an angry roar, shaking their legs and shouting names at Lumpy and me. The Royal Prosecutor glanced at us with a wicked smile. The king ordered silence.

"The defendants' insensitivity to suffering extends even to their own kind, Your Highness," the prosecutor continued. "Routinely, these two children have beaten and bullied their fellow schoolmates, sire. And for no other reason than to cause pain and sorrow and suffering."

The prosecutor paused to let the words linger dramatically in the air.

"Please, go on, madam," the king finally said.

"Your Majesty, I wonder if either of these defendants ever considered how it hurts to receive a hard punch in the stomach from a fellow student twice their size?" the prosecutor asked. "Has either of the prisoners ever wondered how a young boy feels when he is attacked and taunted without cause? Can either of these prisoners honestly say they have ever thought about the trouble caused by their ignorant bullying? No, Your Highness, I submit that they cannot. And I further submit that the defendants therefore deserve the ultimate penalty for their crimes: Death!"

The crowd shouted approval of the prosecutor's words. Lumpy and I looked at each other and trembled. Both of us were in tears from listening to the list of bad things we had done — things that sounded a lot worse than I had ever imagined.

How could we have been so stupid, I wondered. How could we have been so mean for no reason at all? Had we *really* done all those terrible things?

"Thank you, madam, for your skillful presentation of the disturbing facts in this case," the king intoned. "And now it is the prisoners' turn. Do you have anything to say for yourselves after hearing how you have caused so much harm in this world? Do you dare offer any defense?"

"W-well, Your Honor, sir, I — I don't know

what to say, sir," Lumpy said, his lips quivering and tears streaming down his cheeks. "Except I didn't do nothing to hurt anyone. I just thought I was goofing around, you know? Having a little fun, is all. B-but I didn't think I done nothing so bad as what she said, Your Honor, sir! Besides, Freddy's the one that always hated spiders! If you want to kill somebody, it shouldn't be me. It should be Freddy here!"

"Thanks a lot, Lumpy! Some friend you turn out to be!" I said angrily.

I turned to plead for mercy from the king.

"Your Majesty, I feel really awful. I didn't know my behavior had been so stupid and childish. The prosecutor is right about one thing: I never stopped to think about what Lumpy and I were doing. But that's over now, Your Highness. Honest it is! If you'll just let us go back to our families, we'll change for good. We'll be better kids than we were before this happened!"

The mob of spiders hooted and hollered in protest.

"Don't listen to him, Your Highness! He's a

liar!" some of them screamed.

"Death! Give them both death! Death to the liars!" other spiders shouted.

The king listened to his subjects for a moment, then slowly raised his two front legs to ask for order in the hall. Immediately, his subjects fell silent.

"Go on, prisoner," the king commanded.

"Your Highness, please give us another chance to do the right thing!" I begged. "We can't change anything if you kill us. But if you let us go, we can make things better! I won't feel so afraid of spiders anymore! I'm not going to hurt spiders or anything else for no reason — not ever again! Lumpy and I can be nice to Tommy Malloy and make sure no one else ever picks on him. And we can be nice to the other kids in our school, too. *Please*, your Majesty! It's not too late for us to correct our bad ways! Please, grant us mercy!"

The court was quiet as the crowd waited for the king's ruling. His Majesty now would decide if we would live or die.

The king rose slowly to his feet and stood on

the throne of pine needles, his long robe of white spider silk hanging behind him. Lumpy and I glanced at each other, unable to bear the wait as the king pondered our fate.

His eight huge eyes glared down at us. It seemed as if an hour passed before he opened his mouth to speak.

When at last he spoke, he talked loudly and angrily as he passed sentence on his two helpless prisoners.

Even his royal mustache twitched in contempt.

"Your pleas for mercy have touched Our Royal Heart, prisoners. We understand that mistakes are sometimes made through carelessness and ignorance," the king began. "But we cannot find it in Our Royal Self to dismiss your horrible crimes! Your cruelty has surpassed our capacity for compassion! Therefore, it is the ruling of His Royal Highness, the Spider King, that the two prisoners known among humans as Freddy and Lumpy are sentenced to *death!*"

The mob howled with delight and began

chanting "Death! Death! Death!" The king again raised his front legs to demand silence from his subjects.

"The sentence shall be carried out at *once!*" he announced. "Bring in the Royal Executioners! Let the deadly wolf spiders into court so they may seize their victims!"

The enormous tree-bark doors in back of the hall opened. Two spiders entered together — the largest, ugliest, meanest-looking spiders I had ever seen!

Their legs extended far in front of them and their bodies looked massive and strong. They were six feet tall.

Now I knew what a wolf spider was!

The pair of royal killers marched together through the long hall. The crowd cheered as they stalked toward their prey — us!

We were finished this time for sure, I thought. Done for! Doomed!

We were surrounded by giant monsters in the court of the Spider King, somewhere far inside the dark reaches of the earth! And the largest, toughest monsters of all had been ordered to destroy us both!

Lumpy and I were condemned prisoners now, waiting for the final, fatal touch of the Royal Executioners!

Chapter Fourteen

The wolf spiders strode arrogantly through the court, like two bullies on their way to a schoolhouse fight.

"Kill them! Kill the killer kids!" some of the king's subjects screamed.

"Revenge! Revenge! Revenge!" others shouted.

"Cruelty for cruelty! Death! Death!" still other spiders in the mob bellowed.

When the Royal Executioners had approached very near to us, they stopped. Lumpy and I were only two paces away from their long legs and their strong jaws and their sharp fangs.

"*Please!* We don't deserve this!" I shouted at the executioners. "Tell the king to stop! We don't deserve to die!"

"We didn't do nothing," Lumpy pleaded. "Honest! It, uh, must have been, uh, somebody else, guys!"

One of the executioners grinned at Lumpy and me.

"Says *you*! We think you're lying. Besides, you know what they say, kids!" the wolf spider sneered. "You've got to throw your weight around if you want to have any fun! *Ha, ha, ha, ha, ha*!"

The king still stood on his raised throne, looking down at us. Anger gleamed in every one of his eight eyes. Now, very slowly, he sat back down, all of his legs settling under his great, hairy body.

"Bring in the Royal Gallows!" he commanded. "Let our gallows-makers work swiftly now! Hurry! Let this unpleasantness end with the execution of our prisoners!"

Again the mossy, tree-bark doors opened. Three small red spiders quickly marched toward us, walking in step. Two of them dragged sticks with their legs.

At the middle of the hall, the three spiders

came to a sudden stop. Immediately, they began to build the gallows for our execution!

The two spiders with sticks raised them into the air, like goal posts at a football game. The third spider climbed one of the sticks and began to spin a large, sticky web.

As he moved rapidly between the two sticks, building the white net, the king cleared his throat and spoke to us again.

"The condemned prisoners must now hear the horrible details of their fate. They must have this time to understand the final consequences of their actions," His Highness explained.

We squirmed fearfully below him.

"You prisoners will be taken to the web you can see being constructed behind you," the king continued. "This web will serve as your gallows — it will hold you firmly in place for the Royal Executioners! Then you will be eaten by the wolf spiders who serve His Majesty, the Spider King!"

"B-but Your Honor, sir!" Lumpy said. "I don't know much about spiders, yeah sure! But I know spiders like to eat bugs and all, on account of bugs are your favorite food. So wouldn't you and the executioners and everybody like it better if Freddy and me went to catch some juicy bugs for your dinner? Just tell us what you want and we'll bring it to you! Honest!"

"That's true, Your Majesty! We're both really good at catching bugs out in the woods," I added hopefully. "Maybe we could catch enough bugs to feed your whole kingdom, Your Highness, sir!"

"I've listened to enough of your lies and foolishness!" the king answered. "The condemned prisoners shall remain silent! Gallows-makers, are you nearly finished with your work?"

The red spider who was spinning the web paused and turned to face his king.

"Your Highness, work on the gallows is nearly complete," he replied with a bow. "If it please Your Majesty, we shall be done with our Royal task in no more than one minute."

Only one more minute before the monstrous web was built!

Only one more minute before Lumpy and I were trapped there to perish!

Only one more minute to live!

I knew we had to do something now — or die a ghastly death in the mouths of two wolf spiders!

But what? What could we possibly do to get out of this deadly mess?

I tried as hard as I could to remember something from school about spiders — *anything* that might help us escape. I worked my brain desperately, straining to recall any small fact that could save our lives!

Then I remembered my teacher telling us that most spiders actually are *scared* of people! Yes, that was exactly what he said! Spiders usually run away from human beings whenever possible!

Would these huge spiders react in the same way?

I knew that the king's royal workers weren't frightened by Lumpy and me at all — not the Imperial Guard or the prosecutor or the executioners. But maybe, just maybe, the king's *subjects* were afraid of us.

There was only one way to know for sure.

Yes, I now had a wild, crazy idea for our escape attempt. It was all or nothing.

The idea might work.

The idea might fail.

But I knew I'd better find a way to make it work if Lumpy and I ever hoped to leave the Spider Kingdom alive!

Chapter Fifteen

I had to move fast!

Suddenly, I grabbed Lumpy by the hand and tugged him as hard as I could to my left, directly toward the crowd of spiders!

"Come on, Lumpy! Run!" I screamed. "Run for your life!"

We were taking a huge gamble. If it failed, we would probably be eaten alive on the spot by a furious mob of monster spiders!

But the gamble paid off!

The king's subjects did just what I hoped they would do: As we darted toward them, they scurried in all directions to get away from us. They were terrified.

Dozens of spiders of all shapes and colors ran to the right and to the left. They ran to the front of the court and to the back of the court.

They bumped into each other as they scattered to escape the killer kids.

The entire hall was a clatter of chaos, with spiders shouting and hollering as they ran.

"Look out! They're trying to murder more of us!" some spiders in the mob yelled.

"Run away! Run away! The killer kids are loose!" others bellowed.

"Get out while you can! They're going to break off your legs!" still others screamed.

The king was shouting, too.

"*Catch* them, guards! Don't let them escape!" His Majesty ordered. "*After* them! The condemned prisoners *must be punished*!"

This was just the confusion we needed.

Still holding Lumpy by the hand, I ran to the back of the crowd and ducked my head and shoulders low enough to hide.

"Get down, Lumpy!" I whispered firmly. "Maybe the guards won't see us! Come on, stay with me!"

The panicked mob was going wild now. In

their frantic efforts to get away, spiders stepped over other spiders. They pushed and pulled and poked each other. They stomped and lunged and trampled.

And finally they jammed the wide doorway so that no one could get out.

Oh no, I thought. This was *not* good. It was *too much* chaos!

The only possible path to freedom for us was completely blocked! We had no way to escape!

Then one of the Imperial Guards spotted us!

He was a large brown spider with three gold braids around each leg. From the look in his eyes, I could tell he was determined to capture us again for His Highness.

"Coming through! Look out! Move!" the guard commanded, shoving his way through the unruly crowd. "Step away! Move aside, in the name of the king!"

Just one or two spiders separated us from the rushing Imperial Guard.

He stretched his long, brown front legs toward us, reaching out desperately, trying to grab us.

We had to keep running. But we were trapped by the crowd, unable to move even a step. And there was nowhere to go anyway, no way out.

The door was still jammed by the crush of terrified spiders!

We could do nothing but wait for the king's soldier to catch us and return us to the Royal Gallows!

Chapter Sixteen

The soldier of the Imperial Guard was nearly on top of us.

In just another moment he would have us both firmly in his leggy clutches!

That was when a kind of leggy thought came to me — *legs*, I thought, that was it!

The crowd of spiders blocking the doorway also was a crowd of spider *legs*. Maybe Lumpy and I could find a way through the spaces among those legs somehow.

"*Aaaaaggh*!" Lumpy shouted in fear, watching the guardsman approach. "He's gonna get us, Freddy!"

"Follow me, Lumpy! We've still got a chance!" I hollered above the noise of the mob. "Do exactly what I do! Come on!"

Quickly, I dropped to my hands and knees and began to crawl across the green carpet of leaves. Lumpy did the same. Together we moved rapidly across the floor — *through* the spiny, hairy legs of about forty panicked spiders.

"Look out, Lumpy! Move to your right!" I called to him, looking back to check his progress. "No, not that way! Follow me! Come on, Lumpy, crawl to this side! We can make it through here!"

From our level, the tangle of spider legs looked like a thicket of tree trunks. But this strange forest moved constantly.

It was as if we were crawling through a moving maze — hurrying toward a narrow opening among the giant legs, only to watch it suddenly disappear, then racing after a new space between two other spider limbs.

Lumpy and I understood we had to keep going forward, no matter what. We could hear the Imperial Guard soldier fiercely shoving his way toward us through the crowd.

If we slowed down for an instant, if we hesitated or became confused, our escape attempt was lost. We would be trapped by the tangle of legs — and the guardsman would nab us.

"Keep going, Lumpy! Come on, stay with me!" I shouted back to him. "We can do it! Crawl as quickly as you can! Hurry!"

"I'm trying, Freddy! I'm going as fast as I can go," Lumpy yelled. "I'm still right behind you! Get us out of here! I don't want to die!"

We scrambled forward, squeezing our way between the spider legs.

On and on and on and on — we crawled so long that my hands and knees felt bruised and sore.

Finally, we passed through several sets of hairy legs stacked up around the doorway — and crawled out of the Spider King's court at last.

We were free!

Sort of.

Monstrous spiders roamed throughout the huge, dark nest. Even if most of those spiders would run in fear from killer kids, we might bump into members of the Imperial Guard out on patrol.

Besides, soon enough all the king's soldiers would mount a furious hunt to re-capture the condemned prisoners. When word of our escape circulated through the Spider Kingdom, every soldier of the Imperial Guard would be looking for us in every corner of every tunnel in the realm!

Lumpy and I would have to be careful, watching for gold braid around spider legs, keeping away from guardsmen. It was going to be extremely tricky — and extremely dangerous.

We faced another problem, too: We had no idea how to make our way through that endless series of candlelit tunnels!

How would we ever find the hole that would take us back to the outside world? Even if we did stumble across it, how could we ever get out?

I remembered that the deep hole had seemed like a bottomless pit. It would be a long climb up to the woods near our homes, with nothing to pull ourselves up to safety — no ropes, no ladders, nothing to hold on to.

Escape looked nearly impossible.

But we still had to try. Maybe something would turn up that could help us.

So once Lumpy and I had crawled beyond the doorway, through the forest of spider legs, we stood up and began to run.

At least, *I* began to run.

Because when I looked back, Lumpy was standing just outside the doorway, frozen with fear. I hurried back to him.

"Come on, will you, Lumpy! What's wrong with you?" I said. "Are you crazy? We can't stand here! We've got to get going right now! Move!"

"I just c-can't, Freddy!" Lumpy whined. "I c-can't do it, I tell you! You'll have to go ahead without me, I think."

"Do you want them to catch you again?" I shouted. "We haven't got time to play around! Come on, Lumpy! Run!"

"But Freddy, I *can't!*" Lumpy answered. "I can't move!"

"So you're going to be a big, fat pansy now, is that it?" I responded, hoping to make Lumpy angry enough to follow me. "You're going to let yourself be so scared that you can't even run away?"

"No, that's not it, Freddy! You don't get it," Lumpy said. "I think my ankle is broken!"

"What? No, no! It can't be!" I said. "Let me see! Hurry, Lumpy. I think the soldiers are trying to shove through the crowd to follow us!"

When Lumpy exposed his ankle, I could see that it really was injured. It was swollen a little, and slightly black and blue. But I knew his ankle wasn't broken.

Maybe he had turned it while crawling. It was nothing worse than a mild sprain.

"Come on, you can still walk on this. I'll help you," I said calmly. "Just lean on my shoulder for support, Lumpy. We've got to get away while we still have a chance."

Lumpy moaned and whined, but he began to walk. He rested some of his weight on me as he limped through the shadowy tunnel.

I tried to hurry. But we weren't going anywhere fast.

I would take two rapid steps, then feel myself slowed by his foot-dragging heaviness. Two more steps, then I was slowed again by Lumpy's massive weight.

"We've got to walk faster, Lumpy! Even if it hurts," I demanded. "I can still see the door to the court. We're not even out of the first tunnel yet!"

"I'm in pain, Freddy! Ouch! I can't help it!" Lumpy whimpered. "Every time I take a step, it hurts. I'm really sorry. But it hurts! Ow!"

Suddenly, I felt every bit as trapped as when I had been stuck to that giant spider web for so many hours.

What was I going to do?

I couldn't abandon my friend! Even if he had proved that he wasn't much of a friend at all.

If I left Lumpy alone, the Imperial Guard would kill him!

But if I stayed with Lumpy, the Imperial Guard would kill *both of us*!

I was trying to run from a gang of monstrous killers with a two-hundred-pound weight hanging around my neck!

I felt sure Lumpy and I were just like two doomed flies, helpless and soon to become food for spiders.

And there was nothing, absolutely nothing, that I could do about it!

Chapter Seventeen

But there had to be *something* I could do about it.

We couldn't quit now. I put my brain in high gear. I instantly understood we had only three choices:

1) Run faster — but Lumpy *couldn't* do that!

2) Hide — but where?

3) Give ourselves up to the Imperial Guard — and be immediately executed!

As far as I was concerned, that left us only one real choice: We had to find a hiding place. Fast!

I helped Lumpy drag himself out of the long tunnel that led from the court of the Spider King. We were alone in another tunnel now — at least, *almost* alone.

I spotted two small yellow spiders casually walking our way. They hadn't noticed us yet. I ran toward them with a terrifying howl and sent the two of them scurrying off as rapidly as their sixteen legs would carry them.

· I was exhausted from hauling Lumpy around. Sure, I was big and strong for my age, but not *that* big and strong. With his bad ankle, we just could not go any farther.

I had to find some place for us to hide. I started walking.

"Hey, what are you doing, Freddy? Don't leave me here!" Lumpy cried. "I'm your best friend!"

"Yeah, right! Some friend, trying to get the king to kill me so you could save your own neck," I responded. "But don't worry. I'm not leaving you, Lumpy. I've just got to figure out somewhere to hide us for a while."

"Where, Freddy? There's nothing around here except a bunch of long halls," Lumpy said.

He was right. Nothing except the narrow, darkened tunnels.

There was not even a little nook or cranny for us to tuck ourselves into.

We really *were* trapped!

Lumpy couldn't run. Now we couldn't even hide!

Then, the idea came to me! I snapped my fingers.

"I've got it! Lumpy, we've got to *make* some place to hide!" I said. "This is a good spot. It's darker away from those candles. We'll dig our own hole in the wall and climb in there!"

I hurried to Lumpy. Together we limped to a black portion of the tunnel. We began to dig with our hands.

We scraped and scratched first through the spider silk that covered the walls, then through the dirt, clawing at the soil like madmen. We had to make a perfect hole in the wall, something large enough to hold us both but small enough that no passing spiders would notice it.

"Hurry up, Lumpy! Dig faster!" I urged. "The Imperial Guards are going to start looking for us really soon now!"

After maybe three or four minutes of digging, I

could see this was going to be tougher work than I'd imagined. We needed a better plan.

"Look, Lumpy, we're never going to make this hole big enough to hold us both," I said. "We just can't take a chance on digging any longer. Some spider is going to come along and see us. And then that spider will tell the Imperial Guard right where to find us."

"What are we gonna do, Freddy?" Lumpy asked.

"*You're* going to hide here, Lumpy!" I replied. "And *I'm* going to find the opening to the woods that will get us out of this place. I can run through the tunnels quickly by myself. I'll just have to figure out some way to avoid the Imperial Guard — and then hope I can find the right hole."

"OK, Freddy. If you say so," Lumpy answered. "You're the smart one."

For a moment, Lumpy looked meekly satisfied with the plan. Suddenly he stopped and looked at me in alarm.

"Hey, there's a problem," he wailed. "How

will you ever get back and find me again? You'll never remember the way. Please, don't leave me here, Freddy! *Please!*"

He was right. I hadn't thought about finding my way back to Lumpy. It was a big problem.

"Yes," I said. "It's going to be hard to get back to this place. But I'll just have to try and remember the way. That's all I can do, Lumpy."

"No, wait! I have an idea how you can find it," Lumpy said. "Do you have any paper in your pockets, Freddy? Anything! Just some kind of paper."

"Yeah, sure," I said. "I have a huge pack of gum — thirty sticks! So what? How's a gum wrapper going to help us?"

"See, look — you can rip the gum wrappers up into little pieces and drop them while you're running along, Freddy," Lumpy explained. "And you can break up little pieces of your gum and drop them along the way, too. Then you can just follow the trail back to me!"

It was brilliant!

"You're a genius, Lumpy! I won't ever call

you stupid again," I said.

"Uh, thanks, Freddy," Lumpy said, looking surprised that he'd come up with a good idea.

Lumpy crawled into the hole we had dug in the tunnel. It was just big enough to hold him, hiding his large body among the shadows.

I covered the hole back up with the spider silk we had removed.

Then I ran off into the complicated series of tunnels, breaking up little pieces of white gum and silver gum wrapper as I raced on my way. Every thirty or forty yards, I dropped another marker.

I just hoped the pieces were small enough that no one else would notice them!

I rounded a corner from one tunnel to the next, only to find a group of huge spiders meandering on their way somewhere. I ducked back around the corner and waited until they passed, kneeling low to the ground so I was harder to see in the darkness.

Again and again I reached places where I had to go either right or left — forks along my path. Of course, I had no idea which way to go.

I simply guessed, picking a direction at random and hoping I would be lucky enough to find the way out anyhow.

I soon discovered that I *was* lucky. *Very* lucky!

After only about three minutes of running from tunnel to tunnel, I saw a beam of light pouring into the spiders' nest from above. It was an opening!

A hole to the outside world!

It wasn't the same hole I had come down, though — and that's when I realized the spiders had more than one entrance to their nest.

Yes, this was a different hole. A much better hole than the other one!

Because the top of this hole was relatively low. I could reach halfway to it just by extending my hands over my head.

Also, I saw there were a couple of vines and roots sticking out of the dirt nearby, things I could use to help pull myself up. I felt sure I could climb out!

But what about Lumpy? He would never be able to make his way out of the hole, especially with a bad ankle. He was too heavy.

I didn't know how to help him escape.

Still, I had to go back for him. His hiding place wasn't far away. We would get him up to the woods somehow.

Without warning, I saw something shocking. It was heading right at me!

Seven large spiders wearing gold braids around their legs, all members of the Imperial Guard, were running through the tunnel at top speed!

The hunt for the missing killer kids was on — and they had just found one of their escaped prisoners.

Me!

There was only one thing to do: Run away and forget Lumpy!

Horrified by the sight of so many guardsmen chasing me, I leaped for the vines near the hole and pulled with all my strength.

I strained and struggled, wiggling my legs as I tugged myself through the opening — and at last I crawled into the woods.

I had escaped!

I was going to live!

But I had abandoned Lumpy — leaving him alone and lost in the Spider Kingdom for good!

Chapter Eighteen

I knew the spiders could follow me out of the hole. So I kept running!

I ran faster than ever before in my life. I didn't even know where I was going!

Then I remembered a place to hide — the tree fort!

The tree house was broken, sure. But I still could climb into the tree, sitting on some high branches to get away from any spiders that chased me.

And that's exactly what I did.

I sat beside what was left of our fort for an hour or more. Except I didn't see any spiders. Not one.

They hadn't followed me out of their nest, after all.

I really was safe, finally! I could go home —

and tell my parents this incredible tale of horrible giant spiders.

But I couldn't stop thinking about Lumpy. Even if he was a jerk, the poor kid was still in that nest of monsters!

I don't know why, but I just couldn't leave him there — no matter how afraid I was to go back.

I still didn't know how to get him out of the hole, though, even if I *could* find a way to rescue him from his hiding spot.

Then I noticed the long rope and green plastic flashlight lying inside the remnants of our tree house. That gave me an idea.

I grabbed the rope and flashlight, and worked my way slowly down the ladder to the ground. Then I ran all the way back to the Spider Kingdom.

I tied the rope around a large tree near the nest, extending it to the very edge of the hole. I left it there, with no part of it showing below ground.

I lay down on the dirt, poking my head carefully into the nest. I looked to the right and to the left.

No sign of the Imperial Guard — or any other

spiders, for that matter.

Holding the flashlight, I leaped into the hole, wondering if I was crazy or just stark raving mad. Then I followed the trail of shredded gum and wrappers, moving low to the ground, running from shadow to shadow.

It only took me a couple of minutes to reach Lumpy's hideout.

"Psst! Lumpy! Are you still here?" I whispered urgently. "It's me! Come on out! We need to get away right now!"

I watched as first a pair of hands emerged through the spider silk, then a head and finally a body and legs.

"Freddy, where have you been? They're looking for us all over the place," Lumpy said, pulling the sticky spider silk from his hair and clothes.

"It's a long story, Lumpy. I'll tell you later," I said breathlessly. "We've got to hurry if we want to get out of here alive! Come on! I know the way out!"

Lumpy's ankle felt better after his rest inside the little hideaway. But he still limped as we hurried toward the hole. He leaned on me for support as we rushed along.

He knew safety was just a few minutes away, and he did his best to move quickly.

I was amazed that we saw no spiders during our escape. The Imperial Guard must have already searched that part of the nest, I thought. Perhaps they were busily looking for us somewhere else.

Following the chewing gum trail that marked the route to freedom, I had little trouble finding the opening to the woods again. We were nearly rid of the Spider Kingdom.

But Lumpy looked up at the top of the hole with dread.

"Freddy, I can't climb up there!" he whined. "How am I going to get out?"

"Wait here, Lumpy! I have a plan to help you," I said, grabbing the vines and pulling myself out of the hole as I talked.

Once I was above ground, I tossed the end of the rope down to Lumpy.

"Here, tie this under your arms," I called down

to him. "I'm going to pull and you can use your arms and legs to help me. Together, we should be strong enough to bring you up."

But we weren't!

As strong as my muscles were, they weren't enough to handle Lumpy's weight.

I groaned, yanking and tugging on the rope with all my strength. Lumpy grunted, grabbing vines and struggling to get a toehold on the wall of the hole.

"Let's try again!" I cried. "We've got to get you out of there!"

We nearly succeeded. We got Lumpy's body off the floor and started him up the wall of the hole. One of his hands reached out and groped the forest floor.

Then his feet lost their grip, and he tumbled back into the hole.

We tried again and again, straining and sweating, grunting and groaning. No matter how hard we tried, we fell just short of the power needed to drag him out of the hole.

If only there was someone else to help, I

thought desperately. If we just had one more person, we could do it!

"Lumpy, I'm going to run to one of the houses around here and see if I can find somebody to give us a hand," I shouted. "We can't handle this alone!"

"Freddy, wait! *Heeelllp!*" Lumpy screamed from below. "Don't go! There's no time now!"

"What's wrong? Is someone coming?" I asked fearfully.

"Yeah, Freddy! *Everyone* is coming!" Lumpy wailed. "There's about twenty Imperial Guard spiders at the end of this tunnel. They've seen me! They're running this way! *Heeeellllpp!*"

Chapter Nineteen

The flashlight!

I hurried to the hole and threw it down to Lumpy, who caught it one-handed.

His life depended on that old plastic flashlight now!

"What's this for, Freddy?" Lumpy wailed. "Get me out of here!"

"When they get close, shine it in their eyes, Lumpy! They've probably never seen anything like it," I shouted. "If we're lucky, it'll scare them away long enough to get you out. Try to hold them off with that and I'll run for help!"

As I raced toward the nearby houses, I spotted a kid my age walking through the woods. We were saved! I ran toward him dodging trees, waving my arms and calling out.

Then I saw who it was. Tommy Malloy!

The kid I had called a major geek. The kid Lumpy and I had bullied and beaten so often.

Lumpy and I needed him now — in a big way!

"Tommy, come here!" I called. "Please! You have to help me! It's a matter of life or death! Lumpy is trapped and we have to pull him out! Will you help us, *please*?"

Tommy didn't hesitate for a moment.

"Of course I will!" he yelled. "Show me what to do! Let's go!"

Tommy Malloy and I flew through the woods to the rope. Grabbing it tightly, we pulled on it with every bit of strength in our bodies.

"It's working! You're doing it, Freddy! You're pulling me out!" Lumpy shouted from inside the hole. "And the flashlight is holding off the spiders! They're blinded by the light! Pull, Freddy! You've almost got me out of here! *Pull*!"

Puffing heavily, Tommy and I hauled in the rope, one tough handful at a time. We heaved with all our might.

We saw Lumpy's head pop into view!

"Come on, Freddy! I'm almost out!" he shouted. "Keep pulling!"

As I held the rope steady, Tommy Malloy ran to the hole and grabbed Lumpy's arms and helped him climb out of the nest.

We had done it!

With Tommy's help, Lumpy and I had escaped the Spider Kingdom alive.

But we still had no time to lose. The spiders might come after us. Soldiers of the Imperial Guard might pour from the hole at any minute, one after another, to chase the escaped prisoners.

So I took the flashlight Lumpy was holding and threw it into the nest.

That might just be enough to scare the spiders for a few more minutes, I thought. Long enough for us to run home, at least.

And that's just what all three of us did! We ran in three separate directions, as fast as our legs could carry us.

We tore through the woods and down the streets and up our driveways, right to our own homes. And then we all locked the doors and windows and phoned each other to make sure everyone was safe.

I let out a long sigh of relief. It was really over at last!

I felt totally exhausted, though. It was as if I just couldn't hold my head up any longer.

I lay down on the comfortable leather couch in our living room to rest, flicking on the TV before closing my eyes.

I was there just a few minutes, I think, before some startling words filtered through my sleepiness, like a ship's horn piercing a thick fog.

"Spiders are carnivorous creatures whose diet consists mostly of insects," the voice said. "They are no threat to human beings and nearly always run if confronted by people. In fact, spiders often are welcomed into gardens as creatures that help rid flowers and vegetables of pests."

I sat up quickly, looking around to see who was talking. Then I realized the voice was coming from the television. The TV was tuned to a nature program about spiders.

And I had fallen asleep!

Sleep? I shook my head, trying to clear the haze.

It seemed as though I had drifted off to sleep very briefly. And at the same time it seemed as though I had slept for ten years.

To this day, I'm not sure what actually happened to me. My parents insist that I only was dreaming about some place called the Spider Kingdom.

"There's no nest of giant spiders in our woods! You know that, Freddy," Mom scoffs.

I'm not as certain about that as she is. It all seemed so vivid, so real, so terrifying.

Sometimes I'm positive I really was inside the court of the Spider King — even if Lumpy won't admit it. I think he's just afraid people will say he's crazy.

Whether it was a real place or a nightmarish land of my imagination, the Spider Kingdom changed some things in my life.

For one thing, I don't pick on Tommy Malloy now — or anyone else.

Tommy's not my best pal or anything. He's still a little too geeky for me to hang around all the time. But he's a good kid and we've become friends since I've gotten to know him better at school.

I don't spend any time at all with Lumpy these days. I discovered that he really is a jerk, just a troublemaker who's mean to everybody and everything for no reason.

At least I'm strong and large enough that he can't hurt Tommy Malloy anymore. I make sure of that.

Lumpy doesn't pick on anybody when I'm around.

And as for spiders, well I'm *still* not crazy about them, to be honest.

But somehow seeing all those huge spiders made the small ones seem a lot less scary to me. I know now that spiders won't hurt me.

And I won't hurt them either, unless I have to smack one that found its way into my bedroom or some place like that.

Live and let live, that's my motto now.

I know, I know — it probably sounds kind of boring to you, right?

But hey, I still like to have fun! I just found out that you don't have to throw your weight around to do it, that's all.

There are lots of ways to have fun other than picking on kids who can't defend themselves. Or hurting innocent creatures that aren't bothering anything, you know?

Just ask my father, if you doubt me. He'll tell you I still have a really good time.

Too good a time, as far as he's concerned.

See, the other day I kind of got in trouble because I had these firecrackers. I guess I kind of set them off under an empty metal trash can in our driveway, just to hear the loud noise they would make.

It was pretty funny!

Of course, I'll be laughing about it from inside the house for the next week, except for when I go to school.

Dad got a little angry about the firecracker thing — and grounded me for five days.

Oh well! I've still got books to read and TV to watch.

No running around the neighborhood without my parents' permission this time, building tree forts and getting into serious trouble. Not me.

I like to have fun, yeah!

Hey, I'm still a kid. And I hope I never outgrow the need for a good laugh.

But right now, I feel pretty sure I've had enough trouble to last me for the rest of my life!

LET, LET, LET
THE
MAILMAN
GIVE YOU COLD, CLAMMY
SHIVERS! SHIVERS!
SHIVERS!!!

A Frightening Offer: Buy the first *Shivers* book at $3.99 and pick each additional book for only $1.99. Please include $2.00 for shipping and handling. Canadian orders: Please add $1.00 per book. (Allow 4-6 weeks for delivery.)

___ #1 The Enchanted Attic
___ #2 A Ghastly Shade of Green
___ #3 Ghost Writer
___ #4 The Animal Rebellion
___ #5 The Locked Room
___ #6 The Haunting House
___ #7 The Awful Apple Orchard
___ #8 Terror on Troll Mountain
___ #9 The Mystic's Spell
___ #10 The Curse of the New Kid
___ #11 Guess Who's Coming For Dinner?
___ #12 The Secret of Fern Island
___ #13 The Spider Kingdom
___ #14 The Curse in the Jungle
___ #15 Pool Ghoul
___ #16 The Beast Beneath the Boardwalk
___ #17 The Ghosts of Camp Massacre
___ #18 Your Momma's a Werewolf
___ #19 The Thing in Room 601
___ #20 Babyface and the Killer Mob
___ #21 A Waking Nightmare
___ #22 Lost in Dreamland
___ #23 Night of the Goat Boy
___ #24 Ghosts of Devil's Marsh

I'm scared, but please send me the books checked above.

$_____ is enclosed.

Name_____

Address _____

City_____ State_____ Zip _____

**Payment only in U.S. Funds. Please no cash or C.O.D.s.
Send to: Paradise Press, 8551 Sunrise Blvd. #302,
Plantation, FL 33322.**